Dear Parent:
Your child's love of reading

D0091601

Every child learns to read in a different way and at his or her own speed. You can help your young reader improve and become more confident by encouraging his or her own interests and abilities. You can also guide your child's spiritual development by reading stories with biblical values and Bible stories, like I Can Read! books published by Zonderkidz. From books your child reads with you to the first books he or she reads alone, there are I Can Read! books for every stage of reading:

 SHARED READING
Basic language, word repetition, and whimsical illustrations, ideal for sharing with your emergent reader.

 BEGINNING READING
Short sentences, familiar words, and simple concepts for children eager to read on their own.

 READING WITH HELP
Engaging stories, longer sentences, and language play for developing readers.

 READING ALONE
Complex plots, challenging vocabulary, and high-interest topics for the independent reader.

 ADVANCED READING
Short paragraphs, chapters, and exciting themes for the perfect bridge to chapter books.

I Can Read! books have introduced children to the joy of reading since 1957. Featuring award-winning authors and illustrators and a fabulous cast of beloved characters, I Can Read! books set the standard for beginning readers.

A lifetime of discovery begins with the magical words "I Can Read!"

Visit www.icanread.com for information on enriching your child's reading experience.
Visit www.zonderkidz.com for more Zonderkidz I Can Read! titles.

"Honor your father and your mother ..."
—Exodus 20:12

ZONDERKIDZ

The Berenstain Bears® Respect Each Other

Copyright © 2018 by Berenstain Publishing, Inc.
Illustrations © 2011 by Berenstain Publishing, Inc.

This book is also available as a Zondervan ebook.

Requests for information should be addressed to:

Zonderkidz, 3900 *Sparks Dr. SE, Grand Rapids, Michigan 49546*

ISBN 978-0-310-76009-2

Design: Diane Mielke

Printed in China

18 19 20 21 22 /DSC/ 21 20 19 18 17 16 15 14 13 12 11 10 9 8 7 6 5 4 3 2 1

The Berenstain Bears
Respect Each Other

written by
Stan & Jan Berenstain
with Mike Berenstain

ZONDERkidz

It was a beautiful summer day.

The Bear family was going on a picnic.

Mama and Papa packed the picnic.

Brother, Sister, and Honey were ready!

Gramps and Gran were coming too.

"I made my special stew," said Gran.

"Mmm!" said Gramps. "My favorite!"

"Yuck-o!" said Brother.

Sister laughed.

"What did you say?" said Mama.

"Nothing!" said Brother.

"Come on, Sis.

Let's find a good picnic spot."

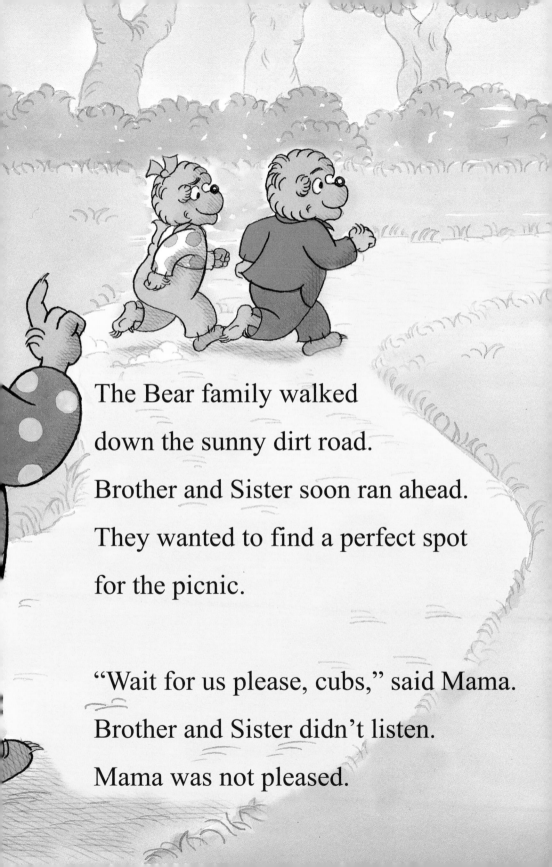

The Bear family walked
down the sunny dirt road.
Brother and Sister soon ran ahead.
They wanted to find a perfect spot
for the picnic.

"Wait for us please, cubs," said Mama.
Brother and Sister didn't listen.
Mama was not pleased.

"There's a good picnic spot
right in these trees," said Papa.
"We used to come here
when I was in school."

"That was a long time ago,"
said Sister. "It looks so old, now!
Let's find a better spot."
Papa was not pleased.

"Here's a lovely spot by the pond,"
said Mama. "Papa and I came here
on our first date."

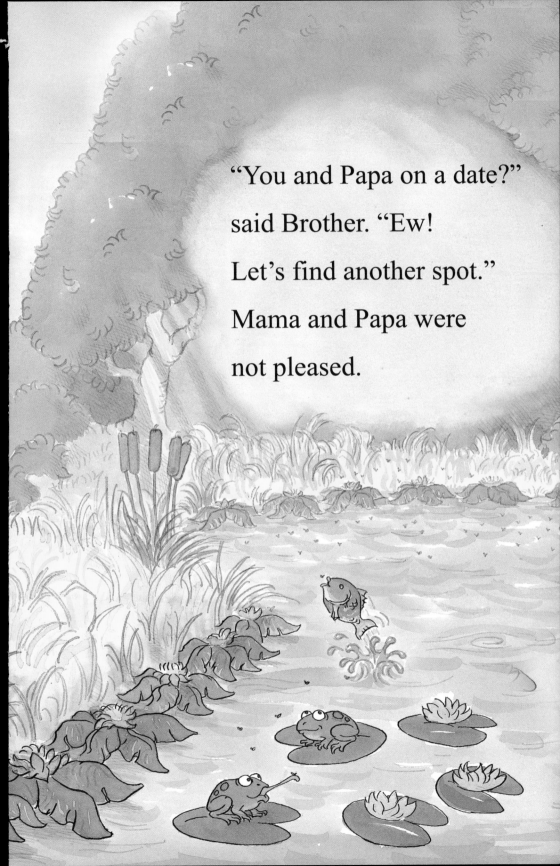

"You and Papa on a date?"
said Brother. "Ew!
Let's find another spot."
Mama and Papa were
not pleased.

"There's a lovely view at the top of Big Bear Hill," said Gran.

But Mama said, "We don't want to climb all that way. Let's find a nicer spot." Gran was not pleased.

The Bear family kept walking.

They were getting hungry,

hot, and tired.

"I have an idea for a picnic spot,"

said Gramps.

But Papa said, "We don't
need help. We know what
we're doing."

Gramps stopped short.

"Now wait a minute!" said Gramps.

"It seems to me you all aren't

showing respect to your elders."

"That's right," Gran agreed.
"The Bible says to listen to those
who are older than you. They have
wisdom to share."

"But, Gramps!" said Papa.

"No 'buts,' sonny!" said Gramps.

"A wise son listens to his father."

"Sonny?" said Brother and Sister.
They had never thought about how
Papa was someone's son.

Brother, Sister, Mama, and Papa

knew Gramps and Gran were right.

"We're sorry!" said Brother and Sister.

"We'll show more respect from now on."

"We're sorry too!" said Mama and Papa.

"We forgive you," said Gran.

"Now come along. Gramps will pick
the perfect picnic spot."

"Yes, indeedy!" said Gramps.

"Where are we going, Gramps?"
asked Brother and Sister as Gramps led
the way.

"Never fear," said Gramps.
"Grizzly Gramps is here!"

The Bear family marched over
hills and through fields.
"Here's the perfect spot!"
said Gramps.

"But, Gramps!" said Sister.

"That's your own house."

"Haven't you ever heard of a

backyard picnic?" said Gramps.

Gramps and Papa fired up the grill.

They heated up Gran's stew.

They grilled salmon too.

They all raised cups of lemonade to show respect for Gramps and Gran.

"To Grizzly Gramps," said Papa.

"He found the perfect picnic spot."

"Mmm!" said Brother and Sister.

"Salmon! That's our favorite!"